Little Hare Books
8/21 Mary Street, Surry Hills
NSW 2010 AUSTRALIA

www.littleharebooks.com

Copyright © Kilmeny Niland 2007
www.kilmenyniland.com

First published in 2007

National Library of Australia
Cataloguing-in-Publication entry
Niland, Kilmeny.
Two tough teddies.

For preschool children.
ISBN 978 1 921272 05 9 (hbk).

1. Teddy bears - Juvenile fiction. I. Title.

A823.3

Designed by Kerry Klinner, Megacity Design
Produced by Pica Digital, Singapore
Printed by Phoenix Offset, China

5 4 3 2 1

One day, an old box was dumped in the park.

Inside were Tilly Ted and Gruffy Ted, squashed among
the other unwanted toys.

'I don't think they're coming back to get us,'
Gruffy said to Tilly. 'They don't want us any more.'

'What will we do now?' asked Tilly.

'We'll have to find someone else to love us,'
said Gruffy.

As the teddies clambered out
of the box, a bird landed nearby
to search for worms.

'Maybe she will love us,' said Tilly.

'Hello, bird,' they said.

The bird didn't see them.
It didn't even hear their little voices.
It just flew away with a wriggling worm.

'Who will love us now?' asked Tilly.

'We'll find someone,' said Gruffy,
'but first they have to be able to hear us.'

So they practised being loud.

Tilly growled at Gruffy.

Gruffy shouted at Tilly.

They growled and shouted until they felt
loud enough to face the world.

Then the teddies went looking for someone to love them.

They peeped between the leaves
and saw a cat with her kittens.

'Maybe they will love us,'
said Gruffy.

'Hello, mother cat!'
they yelled in their gruff new voices.
'Hello, kittens!'

The cats looked up but couldn't see anyone.
All they heard were two tough voices coming from the bushes.

They fled with their tails in the air.

'You see?' said Tilly. 'No one loves us.'

'We'll find someone,' said Gruffy,
'but they have to be able to see us.'

'But we look so scruffy,' said Tilly.
'You have patchy fur and ink stains on your tummy.'

'And your ear is wobbly and your knee needs stitching,' said Gruffy.

'We'll just have to be brave about the way we look,' said Tilly.

So they practised being brave … and bold …
until they felt ready to face the world.

Then the teddies went looking for someone to love them.

Before long they saw a dog.

'Maybe he will love us,' said Gruffy.

The teddies put on their brave new faces
and shouted in their loud new voices.

'HEY, DOG! OVER HERE!'

The dog saw two tough teddies stumping boldly towards him.
He was so startled he ran off with his tail between his legs.

'They can see us and hear us
but still no one wants us,' said Tilly.

The teddies were too sad to keep looking.
They found somewhere to rest and curled up together.

'I have you,' said Gruffy. 'And you have me.'

'Then we really do have someone to love us,' said Tilly.
'We have each other.'

It wasn't long before they were fast asleep.

The teddies didn't hear the ball bouncing past.
They didn't see the little girl running after it.

But Mollie-Sue saw the two sleeping teddies.

They looked so sweet and lovable that she scooped them up in her arms.

Tilly and Gruffy woke with a start.
They were too surprised to be loud or bold or brave.

It didn't matter.

Mollie-Sue hugged them tightly and carried them straight home.

Tilly and Gruffy were
so happy that they didn't
mind being washed …

or dried …

or brushed …

or mended …

or even dressed
in silly clothes.

But sometimes when no one was looking, Tilly Ted and Gruffy Ted
practised being bold and brave and tough ...

just for fun!